For Mum – thanks for all the backup!
C. F.

For Molesey Community Church
S. H.

First published in Great Britain in 2005 by

Gullane Children's Books
an imprint of Pinwheel Limited

Winchester House, 259-269 Old Marylebone Road,
London NW1 5XJ

1 3 5 7 9 10 8 6 4 2

Text © Claire Freedman 2005
Illustrations © Sally Hobson 2005

The right of Claire Freedman and Sally Hobson to be identified as the author and illustrator of
this work has been asserted by them in accordance with the Copyright, Designs and Patents Act, 1988.
A CIP record for this title is available from the British Library.

ISBN 1 86233 552 4

Printed and bound in Singapore

Don't Worry, Mouse!

Claire Freedman ★ Sally Hobson

GULLANE
CHILDREN'S BOOKS

One morning, Cat woke up with one of his famous bright ideas. "Let's go exploring today!" he said to his friend, Mouse.

"Is exploring dangerous?" asked Mouse anxiously.
"'Course not!" Cat replied cheerfully. "But
don't you worry, Mouse – I'll look after you!"

After breakfast, Mouse scampered
upstairs to fetch her straw hat.
Then she and Cat let themselves out through
the gate at the bottom of the garden.
"Which way shall we go?" Mouse asked. "Left or right?"
"You decide!" said Cat. And off they strode
towards the cornfield.

"*Tiddly-diddly-do, explorers we are two!*" sang Cat happily.
"You sound jolly!" neighed Horse.
"Where are you both headed?"

"We're going exploring!" squeaked Mouse. "It's an adventure!"
"Have you brought a map?" said Horse.
"You'll get lost without one!"

"We don't need a map," Cat called. He tugged gently at Mouse's paw and hurried her along before Horse could say another word.

"Cat," said Mouse squeakily after a short while. "I'd hate to get lost. Don't you think we should go back for a map?" "No need to worry, Mouse," Cat replied merrily. "Cats never get lost! Come on!" And on they walked.

Tring-a-ling! Tring-a-ling! Dog pedalled up on his bicycle. "Hello, Dog," Mouse squeaked excitedly. "We're going exploring!" Dog slammed on his brakes and screeched to a halt.

"Exploring, eh?" he barked. "That's hungry work. I hope you remembered to pack some sandwiches!"

Cat waved a paw in the air. "Explorers are far too busy having fun to eat!" he replied. He and Mouse waved Dog *cheerio* and ambled on in the opposite direction.

"Cat, I've been thinking," Mouse piped up, when
Dog was just a dot in the distance. "Perhaps
we should go back for some food!"

Cat calmly picked a buttercup
and tucked it behind Mouse's ear.
"Don't be silly, Mouse," he laughed.
"We'll be home in time for tea."

Cat and Mouse skirted the edge of the field
and stopped for a rest under a shady tree.
Soon Duck waddled over to join them.
"Where are you off to?" she quacked.
"Just exploring!" said Mouse dreamily.
"What – dressed like that!" said Duck.
"Haven't you brought any warm clothes?"

Cat broke off a long blade of grass and blew on it noisily.
"Exploring is hot work!" he said.
Duck waddled away, shaking her head.
By his side, Cat heard his friend sigh.
"What if it suddenly turns cold?" Mouse asked Cat.
"Maybe we should go home and fetch our jumpers!"

"It's much better to travel light!" Cat answered happily. He pulled Mouse to her feet and they both rolled and rolled down the slope and landed in a laughing, tangled heap.

"Hello, what are you two doing?" called Rabbit.
"We're exploring!" giggled Mouse and Cat together.
"I don't see you carrying an umbrella," said Rabbit.
"Look at the stormy sky. If it rains you'll get wet!"

"We'll soon find somewhere to shelter," Cat replied.
He linked arms with Mouse and together they skipped along.
"I like exploring!" trilled Mouse happily. Suddenly she squeaked
with dismay! "Cat, do you hear something?" she said.
Cat and Mouse stood very still and listened.

RUMBLE RUMBLE!

"It's thunder," said Mouse.
"Rabbit was right.
We are going to get wet!"

RUMBLE
   RUMBLE
      RUMBLE!

"Oh no, that was my tummy this time!"
Mouse cried again. "Suddenly I'm cold and
hungry and we don't know where we are!"

"Don't we?" smiled Cat. "Quick, let's
see what's behind the gate!"

Cat lifted the latch to let Mouse squeeze through.
"Ooh, it's a garden just like ours!" squealed Mouse in surprise.
Cat bounded up the garden path, towards the house.
But Mouse was still exploring.

"Hmmm," she said. "That shed looks exactly
like our shed. Even the garden bench is the same,
and the pond too. Wait a minute . . .

. . . we're home!"

Suddenly, the skies opened
and it really did begin to rain.
"Hurry up, Mouse!" yelled Cat from the window.
Quickly, Mouse scurried indoors.

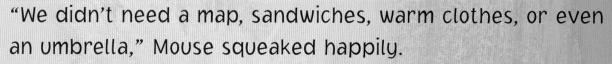

"We didn't need a map, sandwiches, warm clothes, or even an umbrella," Mouse squeaked happily.

"Didn't I promise to look after you?" Cat grinned.

"You did!" Mouse said helping herself to a huge slice of cake.

"And you always do! Let's go exploring again tomorrow!"

"Hmm!" said Cat. Suddenly he had another one of his bright ideas. "Tomorrow, I think we'll go . . . ballooning!"